• NOTE TO CHILD •

Get ready to learn different sounds! Are you excited? You should be. There are more than 50 words with different sounds on the cards beneath this one and you are going to learn them all. Use the pictures to help you learn and be sure to ask questions if you have any.

Are you all set?
Well then, let's

FLIP OVER

to the first new sound and have some fun!

hat
bat

Maggie wore her new blue hat and went out to swing her new red bat.

short a

- Say each word out loud.
- What sound do these words have in common?
- Make up your own sentence using these words.
- What are some words that rhyme with hat and bat?

hat   **bat**

Maggie wore her
new blue hat and
went out to swing
her new red bat.

p|**ig**
w|**ig**

Have you ever seen a little bitty
pig wear a funny brown wig?

short i

- Say each word out loud.
- What sound do these words have in common?
- Make up your own sentence using these words.
- What are some words that rhyme with pig and wig?

pig **wig**

Have you ever
seen a little bitty
pig wear a funny
brown wig?

ice
slice

Nick had a drink with some ice
and a sandwich with a pickle slice.

long i

- Say each word out loud.
- What sound do these words have in common?
- Make up your own sentence using these words.
- What are some words that rhyme with ice and slice?

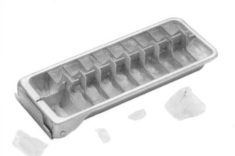

ice **slice**

Nick had a drink
with some ice
and a sandwich
with a pickle slice.

fox
box

Stevie got a toy fox all wrapped up in a shiny yellow box.

short o

- Say each word out loud.
- What sound do these words have in common?
- Make up your own sentence using these words.
- What are some words that rhyme with fox and box?

fox **box**

Stevie got a toy fox all wrapped up in a shiny yellow box.

hose
rose

Grandpa would use the hose to water his favorite rose in the garden.

long o

- Say each word out loud.
- What sound do these words have in common?
- Make up your own sentence using these words.
- What are some words that rhyme with hose and rose?

hose **rose**

Grandpa would use the hose to water his favorite rose in the garden.

ape
grape

The little ape sat in the zoo and ate every single grape he could.

long a

- Say each word out loud.
- What sound do these words have in common?
- Make up your own sentence using these words.
- What are some words that rhyme with ape and grape?

ape **grape**

The little ape sat in the zoo and ate every single grape he could.

goat

coat

John thought the mountain goat must be cold and could use a coat.

long o spelled oa

- Say each word out loud.
- What sound do these words have in common?
- Make up your own sentence using these words.
- What are some words that rhyme with goat and coat?

goat **coat**

John thought the mountain goat must be cold and could use a coat.

crow
snow

It was easy to spot the black crow in the bright white snow.

long o spelled ow

- Say each word out loud.
- What sound do these words have in common?
- Make up your own sentence using these words.
- What are some words that rhyme with crow and snow?

crow snow

It was easy to spot the black crow in the bright white snow.

mug
bug

Martin tipped his mug when he was startled by a little red bug.

short u

- Say each word out loud.
- What sound do these words have in common?
- Make up your own sentence using these words.
- What are some words that rhyme with mug and bug?

mug **bug**

Martin tipped his mug when he was startled by a little red bug.

beach

peach

Each summer I love to sit on the beach and eat a delicious peach.

long e spelled ea

- Say each word out loud.
- What sound do these words have in common?
- Make up your own sentence using these words.
- What are some words that rhyme with beach and peach?

beach peach

Each summer I love to sit on the beach and eat a delicious peach.

sheep

jeep

I can say for sure that I have never seen a sheep driving a jeep.

long e spelled ee

- Say each word out loud.
- What sound do these words have in common?
- Make up your own sentence using these words.
- What are some words that rhyme with sheep and jeep?

sheep **jeep**

I can say for sure that I have never seen a sheep driving a jeep.

light

night

The light in Kate's bedroom helped her sleep at night.

long i spelled igh

- Say each word out loud.
- What sound do these words have in common?
- Make up your own sentence using these words.
- What are some words that rhyme with light and night?

 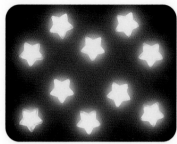

light **n**ight

The light in Kate's bedroom helped her sleep at night.

snail
nail

Dan saw a snail leave a trail
that was as thin as a small nail.

long a spelled ai

- Say each word out loud.
- What sound do these words
  have in common?
- Make up your own sentence
  using these words.
- What are some words that
  rhyme with snail and nail?

snail **nail**

Dan saw a snail
leave a trail that
was as thin as a
small nail.

pink

sink

Ali was cleaning her paintbrush
and got pink paint all over the sink.

nk

- Say each word out loud.
- What sound do these words have in common?
- Make up your own sentence using these words.
- What are some words that rhyme with pink and sink?

pink **sink**

Ali was cleaning her paintbrush and got pink paint all over the sink.

fish
dish

Mike's fish, Lefty, liked it when
Mike set his bowl upon a blue dish.

sh

- Say each word out loud.
- What sound do these words have in common?
- Make up your own sentence using these words.
- What are some words that rhyme with fish and dish?

fish **dish**

Mike's fish, Lefty, liked it when Mike set his bowl upon a blue dish.

sp|**oon**

m|**oon**

Liz licked the ice cream from her spoon as she eyed the moon.

oo

- Say each word out loud.
- What sound do these words have in common?
- Make up your own sentence using these words.
- What are some words that rhyme with spoon and moon?

sp|oon m|oon

Liz licked the ice cream from her spoon as she eyed the moon.

bed

sled

Jimmy believes that Santa Claus has a bed shaped like a sled.

short e

- Say each word out loud.
- What sound do these words have in common?
- Make up your own sentence using these words.
- What are some words that rhyme with bed and sled?

bed **sled**

Jimmy believes that Santa Claus has a bed shaped like a sled.

nurse

purse

Betty the nurse always seemed to forget her purse.

ur

- Say each word out loud.
- What sound do these words have in common?
- Make up your own sentence using these words.
- What are some words that rhyme with nurse and purse?

nurse **purse**

Betty the nurse always seemed to forget her purse.

sock
clock

Joe looked for his other sock, but the clock showed that he was late.

k spelled ck

- Say each word out loud.
- What sound do these words have in common?
- Make up your own sentence using these words.
- What are some words that rhyme with sock and clock?

sock **clock**

Joe looked for his other sock, but the clock showed that he was late.

house
mouse

Auntie Ann could not stay in her house once she saw that mouse.

ow **sound spelled** ou

- Say each word out loud.
- What sound do these words have in common?
- Make up your own sentence using these words.
- What are some words that rhyme with house and mouse?

house **mouse**

Auntie Ann could not stay in her house once she saw that mouse.

ring
string

I have a small ring that I tied around my neck with some string.

ng

- Say each word out loud.
- What sound do these words have in common?
- Make up your own sentence using these words.
- What are some words that rhyme with ring and string?

ring **string**

I have a small ring that I tied around my neck with some string.

toy
boy

Rupert's toy truck was the sort of toy owned by many a boy.

oy

- Say each word out loud.
- What sound do these words have in common?
- Make up your own sentence using these words.
- What are some words that rhyme with toy and boy?

toy **boy**

Rupert's toy truck was the sort of toy owned by many a boy.

locket

rocket

Diana had a neat locket that was made from the metal of a rocket.

ck in the middle of a word

- Say each word out loud.
- What sound do these words have in common?
- Make up your own sentence using these words.
- What are some words that rhyme with locket and rocket?

locket **rocket**

Diana had a neat locket that was made from the metal of a rocket.

math
bath

Hank was such a good student that he even liked to do math in the bath.

th

- Say each word out loud.
- What sound do these words have in common?
- Make up your own sentence using these words.
- What are some words that rhyme with math and bath?

math **bath**

Hank was such a good student that he even liked to do math in the bath.

lime
dime

When Al went to the store to buy a lime, he found out that it cost a dime.

long i

- Say each word out loud.
- What sound do these words have in common?
- Make up your own sentence using these words.
- What are some words that rhyme with lime and dime?

lime **dime**

When Al went to the store to buy a lime, he found out that it cost a dime.

Below are half of the words you have helped your child to read. Notice that they are not broken up by sound as they are on each individual card.

Help your child read each of these words again. Instruct him or her to come up with new sentences using each pair of words.

Let's Review!

hat	bat	goat	coat
pig	wig	crow	snow
ice	slice	mug	bug
fox	box	beach	peach
hose	rose	sheep	jeep
ape	grape	light	night

hat	bat
pig	wig
ice	slice
fox	box
hose	rose
ape	grape
goat	coat
crow	snow
mug	bug
beach	peach
sheep	jeep
light	night

Once again, help your child read the other half of the words he or she has just learned.

This time, in addition to creating new sentences for each pair of words, also have him or her mix and match all the words to come up with slightly more complex sentences.

Let's Review!

snail nail

pink sink

fish dish

spoon moon

bed sled

nurse purse

sock clock

house mouse

ring string

toy boy

locket rocket

math bath

lime dime

GOOD JOB!